The wheels on the bus go round and round,
Round and round, round and round.
The wheels on the bus go round and round
at the zoo.

The bear on the bus goes brum brum brum,
Brum brum brum, brum brum brum.
The bear on the bus goes brum brum brum
at the ZOO.

The penguin on the bus goes flip flap flop,
Flip flap flop, flip flap flop.
The penguin on the bus goes flip flap flop
at the ZOO.

The warthog on the bus goes snort snort sneeze,
Snort snort sneeze, snort snort sneeze.
The warthog on the bus goes snort snort sneeze
at the zoo.

The hippos on the bus go squish squash squeeze,
Squish squash squeeze, squish squash squeeze.

The hippos on the bus go squish squash squeeze at the zoo.

The tyres on the bus go *hiss* **BANG** pop!

Hiss **BANG** pop! *Hiss* **BANG** pop!

The **tyres** on the bus go *hiss* **BANG** pop! at the zoo.

The creatures on the bus tip upside down,
Upside down, upside down.
The creatures on the bus tip upside down
at the zoo.

The meerkat on the bus goes slip slip slide,
Slip slip slide, slip slip slide.
The meerkat on the bus goes slip slip slide
at the ZOO.

The tiger on the bus goes
ROAR ROAR ROAR,
ROAR ROAR ROAR,
ROAR ROAR ROAR.

The tiger on the bus goes
ROAR ROAR ROAR
at
the
ZOO.

The **croc** on the bus goes

SNAP SNAP SNAP,

SNAP

SNAP

SNAP,

SNAP

SNAP

SNAP.

The **croc** on the bus goes

SNAP SNAP SNAP

at

the ZOO.

The skunk on the bus goes stink stink stink,

Stink stink stink, stink stink stink.

The skunk on the bus goes

stink

stink

stink

at

the

zoo.

The **owl** on the bus goes blink wink blink,
Blink wink blink, blink wink blink.
The **owl** on the bus goes blink wink blink
at the **ZOO**.

"Everybody off.
No pushing please!"

The jumbo on the bus goes puff puff puff,
Puff puff puff, puff puff puff.
The jumbo on the bus goes puff puff puff
at the ZOO.

The **creatures** on the bus go clap clap clap,
Clap clap clap, clap clap clap.
The **creatures** on the bus go clap clap clap
at the zoo.

All aboard!
All aboard!
And off we GO!

The **wheels** on the bus go **round** and **round**,
Round and **round**, **round** and **round**.

The wheels on the bus go **round** and **round** at the **ZOO**.

For Rafe Peacock – J.W.

For Tamlyn, Caroline and Alison
who keep the wheels going round – A.S.

PUFFIN BOOKS
Published by the Penguin Group: London, New York,
Australia, Canada, India, Ireland, New Zealand and South Africa
Penguin Books Ltd, Registered Offices: 80 Strand, London WC2R 0RL, England
puffinbooks.com
First published 2012
001 – 10 9 8 7 6 5 4 3 2 1
Text copyright © Jeanne Willis, 2012
Illustrations copyright © Adam Stower, 2012
All rights reserved
The moral right of the author and illustrator has been asserted
Made and printed in China
ISBN: 978–0–141–33011–2